Shannon,

Thanks for all of your interest in the writing club! I'm so glad you are going to be an officer next year!

Best Wishes,
N. Drypte
5/16/09

Secrets of the Veil

There is a light that shines above,
Below, a shadow swathes that love.
Time shall take me far away,
The veil shall keep me there to stay.

This book is a work of fiction. No portion of this book may be copied, photo-copied, transmitted or stored electronically or otherwise without the express permission of the publisher and author, except for small references for the purpose of reviewing the book on-line or in print. To obtain permission to quote, please contact:

SF Communications of Georgia
P.O. Box 1311
Clarkesville, Georgia 30523

www.sfcommunicationsgeorgia.com
Phone: 706-499-3914
Email: staff1@windstream.net

To contact the author:

Nicholas Gupta
Email: ngupta@nicholasgupta.com
www.nicholasgupta.com

Cover design by Digital Impact Media, Don Bagwell, Cornelia, Georgia.
Published April 2009

1 2 3 4 5 6 7 8 9 0

ISBN # 978-0-9650478-9-0
Printed and distributed in the US by Lightning Source, Inc.

US $12.95

Secrets of the Veil

by
Nicholas Gupta

Also by Nicholas Gupta...

The Unknown Species

DEDICATION

To Amanda Nye, the Aunt Aman-dieu

To Emily Gupta, who knew. Everything.
and
To Coach John Williams; GOLDEN RODS!

PREFACE

Writing this book was painful. I experienced such mental and emotional trauma. I wanted to cover a psychological theme that could connect to people. *Secrets of the Veil* is disturbing and dark. When writing the vignettes, I would have to change my usual, positive mind-set, and utilize a negative, unpleasant emotion. To gather the book's words, I would have to venture to a sad, upsetting world and collect them.

Some of the ideas and concepts covered in this novel I based on certain events. Following the completion of *The Unknown Species*, my debut novel, I decided that I was ready to explore a different genre, one that was not as fantastical. My sophomore year of high school began, and there were events that gave me inspiration to write a book with this theme. While I do not subscribe to some of the dark concepts presented in this novel, I needed to force myself to view these ideas with a darkened eye and thrust them forcefully at my readers. The mood of my writing, therefore, is morbid. My purpose is simply to get the reader to think. I do wish for them to be interested in these thought-provoking ideas, and for them to press forward, to analyze differences between the concepts.

In addition to the emotional calamity, I also suffered severe writer's block half-way through the project. Visuals and music—an important fundamental in the production of my writing—became tasteless and unhelpful. Stress in school really did not assist my clouded mind, either. On the weekends, when I aimed at writing, I would spend hours trying to write just a paragraph. An associate gave me tools to help with my difficulties, but they did not seem to work. I was anxious, tense, and erratic. Later, I did improvisations and other acting exercises as well as meditation to help me. I also talked to people, and interacted with them on a deeper level.

This book was an interesting transition from the ambiguous plot of *The Unknown Species* to a more brutal, realist theme. I do hope you see the value in it and can use its concepts to think deeper about life situations. Before closing, I would like to thank my friends, associates, and family, those people who were encouraging, kind, and helpful during this time. I greatly appreciate those wonderful people!

Nicholas Gupta
2009

PROLOGUE

My mortal body contains an immortal soul. And for years, my soul was purged by the veil. From my internal conflict, from my endless suffering, my conscious mind was forced to regress within a new world ruled by a veil. My mind sent me to a world of illusion, one embedded in a passage of Time. That was where my soul was tortured, and my body was harmed by evil. Although this conjured world was seemingly non-existent, my entire mortal body was delivered to that place of darkness. I saw it all. I learned to survive there. I became trapped within that world. I had cast myself into the dark shadows of Time.

It was my fault. I was afraid. Scared. I felt myself being pushed away from the warm world that I was used to. My new world, a twisted, fiendish piece of inhumanity, barely clung onto the edge of reality. It was a world of darkness, evil, betrayal, and sadness. I thrived only on thoughts of shadow, those that were inanimate and unpromising. The words I spoke were dry, unnatural, and trite. They were laced with particles of ambiguity. My name meant nothing. My name—a string of syllables! No emotion, no image, no importance.

Veils, obstructions in the passages of Time, solely exist because of the foibles of humanity. Lies, illusion, evil, secrets. These factors take forms of velvet veils that hang in the jointing chambers of Time. They cloak out all light. They cloak out all reason. They cloak out all truth. The veil was the guardian of the place where I was sent, my place in the passages of Time that was cursed by darkness. The essence of time is captured, formulated, and organized to structure life. Interconnecting passages of time join lives together. And there were many instances when I found a veil between my life and the life of someone else.

I regressed within a world of a veil for eternity, it felt. It was fear that guided me to that place. The place was not accessible to all mortals. It was a sacred realm of Time. I was trapped in one of Time's numerous intertwining ducts. It was cold, dangerous and lonely there. Others have their own veils. Others have their own worlds. And these worlds—these worlds that are commanded by veils—are purely structured by illusion.

Within the void of the veil, I was expecting flavors of safety and reassurance to curb my fear and loneliness. But the veil has its own secrets. Its command made it easy for my mind to sweep me away from the world of reality and bring me to a place of illusion. There I faced new things. There I saw, touched, and felt things that no other mortals could even grasp. My weak soul was split into pieces and enslaved by dark emotion.

My story is faintly told within the pages of this book. Fragments of my story are loose, dying, and struggling to find the light. The darkest chapters of my life—the darkest concepts of humanity—were branded onto my soul by the veil. I choked during consumption of these overwhelming ideas. I struggled to handle such disturbing feelings. The secrets of the veil, the secrets of evil, now present my tortured soul. My tale can barely be seen from these secrets of darkness. My past—my story—is scarred by their ideals.

Part One
Torture

A key to the heart, the sight of the mind, and a passage to the soul... are all inside.

I woke up on a stone floor. The ground was chiseled. Strange markings were carved on the surface. The Codes of Time were engraved within these passages! On the muddy stone walls beside me, more codes. They glowed with a jade light. This place, these passages, are not meant for mortals. The answers here are private.

At times I look up. I peer toward what I hope to be a limitless area of sky. But it is confined. It is a brick, rigid structure, obstructing my view
of the heavens.

What slumbering evil dwells here?

In fear, his face was hidden by the veil's violet curtain. An uncertain eye was covered. He lost himself. He lost himself within a world of fear.

Out from music and sound came color
and form! But the veil diminished all.
Nothing remained once it swept
me away.

Silence filled the world. Silence filled the void of sadness.

I heard among the bustle of loneliness a laconic din.

A frigid breeze blows the veil, and the curtain slowly sways back and forth. This wind… it stings my eyes, they are dry and bloodshot. No rest, no peace, nothing. Nothing is left here. Nothing but a hoarse wind and the veil of darkness.

This chamber of the veil, it is dangerous. Shards of glass blow around in the freezing wind. Thick thorns grow out of the stone floor. The veil commands this scourge of man!

The deafening silence was tormenting me. The unspoken words originating from nowhere cursed me. They were there, they were gathering around me. And as I reached out to garner a bit of light to keep me safe, I failed to collect anything but shadows.

Who is this man who hides his face? I see him,
watching me intently. He knows me, while
I cannot identify him. His face is blurry, his
presence shadowed. It is shadowed by the
distortion of the veil. So in what way can I
help myself to see his face correctly? I cannot
stand above the veil, I will not pass through it.
I will not betray it, I will not destroy it.
The veil is mine, the veil is mine. It is all
that will keep me from
the pain of reality.

They suffered endlessly, not due to external dilemmas, but simply because of the intrapersonal issues that scarred their lives.

And what was left within him?
Nothing.
Nothing, save the many secrets of evil.

The weak shall always regress within the shelter of the veil. And they sit there, trembling under the might of illusion, like fools. And once their worlds have finally collided, they emerge from the darkness, now pawns of evil.

I was upset to learn that there was no interest. I was upset to learn that he didn't offer support. All that was with me was a surfeit of discouragement, so beautifully contained by the veil of isolation.

The integrity of light kept her soul pure and free. But I never lived a life so perfect. My words were never blessed with light. They were never proofed and corrected. They always seemed to retain characteristics of darkness and detachment...
characteristics that, in turn, removed me farther and farther away from reality.

Can you keep a secret? Can you keep private truths away from the clutches of enlightenment? Who can I turn to? To whom can I lend these words of secrecy?

Something ordinary, something usual, will fit. It stretches across the void of fear and keeps all balanced. However, the veil does not feel. The veil does not obey a command for comfort. The veil's mind simply spews out the action that is fastest. This action, it is not placating to the human mind. It is unbearable. Without the comfort of something ordinary humans who dwell close to the veil shall suffer.

I remember the biggest mistake I ever made. I stood up and strode right toward the veil of illusion, the veil of darkness, and got my hand ready. I was ready to reach through the veil, and discover what was on the other side. The veil's velvet curtain was soft on my dry fingers. And eventually, my hand passed through it. Warmth. Warmth was all that I felt. It felt so intriguing! I smiled and looked at the veil. But that faded slowly as I noticed its violet shade becoming darker and darker. It seemed to threaten and intimidate me, but the warmth on the other side was too enjoyable. Until I felt excruciating pain. Something on the other side was slicing at my hand. I screamed in fear and withdrew my hand from the veil.

It was bleeding. It was mutilated.

The veil had hurt it.

His one place, his one sanctuary, became infested with evil. The gorgeous and safe room became festered with minions, workers who forever slaved within the burning world of Hell. The last safe place... desecrated! His truths... altered! His safety... gone!
These were his new realities.
Everything else had faded away.

These innocuous actions, those that brought forth an air of safety, seemed to transform. Everything has an inverse. Every great thing has a dark perspective. And the actions themselves lost their unequivocal beneficence, and instead took on a new,
well-seasoned taste of evil.

Among the moments of full ease and kindness, for some reason, in some way, calamity could be felt. Animosity was sensed. But there was not a method to atone for such confusion. So, waiting for more, idle until the answer came along, they both refused to face its entirety.

The pain of nature could be read. It was evident and visible. There were gashes in plants, small inconsistencies within the patterns of growth, and decay on the ground where hatred had once walked the earth.

The fire, a burning vessel of destruction, raged endlessly throughout the forests of tranquility. In a matter of seconds, it voraciously consumed the majestic nature that had been flourishing for eternity.

There was a twisted smile upon her face.
It was a smile of pure malevolence. Her
mind was grappled by evil. Her actions
left a wake of cruelty. Her eyes cast a
lurid glow—eyes doused
with crimson flames.

The sedulous anger was always existent. It did not disperse, fade, or lose its intensity. The anger was preserved within his mind of vengeance. And the veil assisted him. It ensured that the anger would never leave his world of desperation. The anger would never leave the sad, dark world that he now called home.

Let me out.
Oh please, let me out of here!

People pass through the veil, and they disappear. Shadows trail behind them as they cease to exist.

Is there but one word you can speak to
me? Is there but one syllable
that can revive me?
Please... do help me.

The war goes on and on. Lives are tossed into the chasm of combat, and never get out. Hundreds have fallen. Hundreds are dead. They are gone. More and more mortals are thrown in and never return. And the war, it goes on.

I waited. I waited... without direction, knowledge, or prediction. And then the dark moment crept into the passage of Time, and overwhelmed my unprepared mind.

The horrible conflict between the two friends stemmed from a battle of veils. At different times, at different places, different emotions were outlined. Both of their faces were constantly changing and shifting. A logical, basic definition of their feelings was scarcely readable.

Insidious plots were a main product of the veil. Anguish sweeps over its victims. They writhe and sprawl on the floor of the room. They are in a world of pain and suffering. And every single one of them has failed to get out.
The veil does not allow it.

I grew tired of his mind games. I grew impatient with his lack of reason. I lost tolerance for his hesitation. And from this, I altogether found myself being pushed away, all due to the animosity that had spawned between us.

The dark path taken, the evil action completed, the sad choice made. While he was in control of all of them, they all affected me. They crossed into my determined path, and caused me to have to change direction. Parts of my life were cursed by his actions. And I struggled to cleanse my mind of those happenings. Atonement was a necessity for me. The amber fire must be dowsed. But there was no water available.

Societal pressures, insecurities, fear! He stole away all hope and reason, and extinguished them. So much potential... unfulfilled! In very little time, he moved to the other side of himself, away from the reality of emotion, and left me behind. The growth of friendship is a trembling tower, precarious and risky.

If I become happy, if I am full of joy, I find myself becoming more prone to bad occurrences. Happiness is seemingly vulnerable. It passes on, and revisits at another time. While veneration achieves personal enlightenment and upgrades a soul to a heightened state, the exultation of happiness is only a temporary source of emotional height.

From my fear I find a new feeling. It is betrayal. I feel as though the veil has betrayed me. It would have kept me safe—
I would have been fine!
All is different, though.
The veil is my torture.

The veil crushed his soul and weathered his body. His radiant eyes were milky, his sight was weakened, and his mind—it had been taken over.

When I die, a single soul will remain. It will reside here, alone. The world has shunned me. Light has left me.
I am lonely.
Danger. Sadness. Darkness.
These are surrounding me.
These have become me.

His mind became plagued. Darkness and evil spread throughout him, like a virus. The poison of the veil, the evil of the veil. His eyes twitched with confusion, his entire source of logic completely gave out, and he fainted without it. And upon his awakening, upon his revival into a different world, a new source of logic would be present. One entirely ruled by the veil of illusion.

A grievous tear in the tender threads of the mind had occurred. Oblivion wove its intricate pattern into the structures of intellect, and corrupted the human psyche.

A horrible transformation occurred. The weak human had been taken over. Her soul had been encroached on for some time, and now the veil had infiltrated it. The veil's dark matter spread throughout the mind of the mortal, and eradicated all. Without a central source, her body morphed, and became misshapen. The final threads of humanity were sluiced out of her unconscious body, and a dark minion was formed. A minion led evil, despair, and insanity.

The veil shall always keep the curious away from truth, reality, and enlightenment. If they strain to see past, if they attempt to see through the violet cloak, they must be kept back. Curiosity, a blind source of knowledge and discovery, will disrupt the impending darkness. It will create a flame, a change, a light. Light that will dilute the shadows.

Part Two
Enlightenment

You see, the veil becomes you.
If one dares to battle the veil,
one battles himself.

It was disturbing, insane, and flagrant. Atrocity swarmed, and feelings of anguish became prevalent. A single event, a single scandal shook the world, and debauched minds. It took only one person to cause such madness.

Only a trace of harmony remained.

Why do the bad things always happen to those who work so hard, those who try their best, and those who to resist such misfortune?

I have seen things that scar my eyes. I have seen a dead human. I have seen a fatal explosion. I have seen a sacrifice. For a few months I was cast away from my favored world of prosperity and harmony. I touched a world of silence, a world of tumult, a world of ends. Ends that mark the evils of Man.

He dreamt nonstop. With his imagination, he lapsed into grand reveries. A world of color. A world of light. A world... of love. A world of perfect atonement awaited him in his dreams.

If you do not examine the injury, if you do not carefully clean and inspect the emotional wound, then it will become infected... simply because of a refusal to help it heal properly. A bandage alone will not hold back the full potential of pain.

Unnecessary details always seem to have a way to weigh situations down. Why do we dwell on such rash emotions? These emotions... they are unstable, tasteless, and weak. But somehow, they succeed in bringing forth massive amounts of confusion.

I do suppose that I have intentionally swept away traces of my past. I have chosen to live a life of mystery. I like it that way. Only those who reside near me will know the truth. But the others, the others will succumb to the veils that block my face.

The man was draped in shadow. He was unable to be identified. Moving through the channels of Time, this man disembarked one train and boarded another. What was he looking for? Who was his target? No one knew. And no one could learn either. The man surrounded himself with agents of distortion, solely to keep his mind isolated, and his face hidden from the eyes of others. That is how he preferred it.

It was a tale of mystery.

To be seen, to be viewed in ways that we, as humans, request, one must not demand it, but create it. And therein lies the secret of true prestige... only alacrity will take one toward the zenith.

We here hold the ability to create, to breathe life into dying ideas, and to formulate crucial inventions. But that is not all that we possess. We have the ability to destroy. We have hatred. We have war. We have the fundamentals of death that can bring an end to all worlds. And when all collapses, we will disappear along with it, until nothing remains.

The perfect human, left alone at the end of Time, left alone within a dead world, will endure a test. It is a battle of will. Does he possess the skills to exist and remain? Yes. Yes they do. The perfect human, left alone at the end of Time, has the potential to create a world of his own.

The denouement, the outcome, the ending. All are listed within the passages of Time. Secrets of the end were coded, written in forms that only the ancients could interpret, and filed away within the Library of Life. The mortals weren't to discover what was to lie ahead.

The end is but a simple chapter, a concluding segment, one whose purpose achieves great popularity. But paucity was looming. None had the abilities to see the secret path that they were going to follow. And in a world of greed, fear, and a necessity of knowledge, those people suffered the scarcity of truth. The desire for knowledge, it seems, is insatiable.

The human body is but a useless puppet. The body bleeds, takes on illness, and altogether loses its efficiency with age.
What is worthwhile?
It is the hidden factors of the human that are the worthwhile features. It is simply the soul, the mind, the thoughts.
Those that create identity.

You let every aspect of your life affect you. And sometimes you need to be willing to lay all aside to make things work. Otherwise your actions will be based on a distorted past.

Lies are vessels of illusion that contaminate the truth and shun the light.

Lies can make people seem who they are not, lies can add a quietus to an interminable story, and lies can put a misleading light in a world of shadows. The powers of lies—they are unfair. They are deceptive. And although they can make things appear better, they will never last. This characteristic is inevitable. It is simply the lie's mortality in the world of reality.

He searched forever. He searched all dimensions and worlds. But he never could find her. He never could find the one he truly loved.

It was just so... tasteless!
Such a tasteless love was all that
kept the two together.

I do not believe in perfect love. Sure, there is interest, support, titillation, and affection. But love? No. Humans are so wrong for each other! They try and try and fail and fail. But what is that factor? What is that factor that refuses to let them come together? Is it one of a veil?

For seven years I spoke with God. He told me... everything. God told me all the mistakes he made. All the evil he dropped onto my world. He spoke to me of the curses he lavished upon the human race. And God whispered to me in fear. He whispered to me about the stains of darkness that left scars in the world.

When I saw God, I was expecting to see a being of light. A being of supremacy. A being of omnipotence. But when the veil was lowered and I could see correctly, I saw... a hideous spirit. It had grotesque wings. It had vermilion eyes. The phantasm did not speak. It did not reveal those long-awaited secrets of the world that I was hoping to learn about. It simply watched me with contempt, reflecting the decay of my tortured soul.

I wish to question the equity of power. Who are they to lead us? Who are they to control us? All minds are tied to the timeline of life. And all lives cruise on the road of existence. All is one, unifying body. So who has such power to create the detours?

Upon the road of existence, there is constant change. Lives are constantly coming and going along their timelines. Some roads are paved, while others are rugged and incomplete. Life can be smooth, and life can be difficult.

There are constantly accidents and mishaps, as different lives collide and open up new sectors of the timeline. Absolute, strong-willed people emerge from the unified body, and clash with the other values and stories of another person. The timeline shall never end.

Trust is an illusion. Boundaries for knowledge are non-existent. One to confide in... false! One to share everything with... dangerous! These curses of reality show the true cons of Man. Worlds collide. People choose. Secrets are released into an insecure society, and scattered. They settle uneasily atop constantly moving minds. Nothing is rigid. Nothing is sealed. Nothing is promised.
But one thing is certain.
All decisions made here are unsafe.

Definitive answers. The words that possess strength. Orders of the divine. They are so powerful that they can break through illusion, shadows, and darkness. Without these active terms, the veil will rule over the speaker. But with integrity and will, the veil shall have competition!

They all looked at me, dumbfounded. All of them lacked a way to see the light I had shed upon them. And once I accepted the fact that I was too far above them, too far away to remain at their level of thinking, I simply remained silent.

The weight of the world was supported by his supreme emotion. His anger cast into the oceans and scorched the water. The flowers struggling to emerge from the earth shuddered. Man's structures dissolved into gray soot. Flames of death scarred the barren world, and all humans vanished.

Humans! Such fools! Such vessels of contamination! They run on tangents of ignorance. They are graced with arrogance! Their struggling thoughts are bundled together like a heap of refuse. These thoughts, they are bland and gray, and should be kept far, far away.

They have made a mistake. They have made an error. They have torn a hole in the quilt of logic. Now I am furious. I will crush them! They have offset the correct situation. They have offset the proper balance. And because of that, they shall all suffer. Every single one of them!

Let's take away that make-up and let's take away those stilts. Then we can see how amazing you really are! You wear a mask! You cover your face with a veil! And everyone looks at that illusion, bends down, and praises your false excellence.
Not me though.
I know who you really are.

With my anger, I shall set the world on fire, and all will be doomed.

*Et maintenant je regarde un monde de puissance!
Un monde de guerre, de sang,
et des citoyens sans mots.*

The world shall know of what you have done. The whole world shall know of the decision you have made. They will know that you are responsible for his untimely end. And the whole world shall forever stymie your desired amends.

Part Three
Escape

He extended his arm and aimed it at the
evil. His natural divinity trailed behind
him. This hero... this leader. He stopped
the whirlwinds, he stopped the firestorms,
he stopped the cons of Man. The hero
opened the few portals of light,
and cleansed the dark world.

A divine soul must make a choice, and lead all. One man. One woman. One child. They will be chosen. They must stand above the veil, and make their choice. Who to leave behind... who to bring forth. The ones left behind will die and fall into the clutches of the veil. The ones brought forth... they shall meet judgment.

With poise, benevolence, and integrity, the speaker delivered knowledge. And the weak scattered around the bright light cast from him. They fed off of this light, they grew and became astute. Their wills were stronger, and in turn, these developing people were bound by their own command. The words of the divine one raised the weak from deep within the veil, and rested their minds on a platform above it. These trembling, dangerous creatures left that cursed place, and thrived on good.

Equity's hands reached through the portal of darkness and seized the dispute. It wrangled and twisted it, forming a new situation, a brand-new look, one that was completely different. And from that moment, the veil's grasp had weakened. Logic had gotten inside.

The fearless warrior gleamed like light. As attacks from others landed upon him, the warrior staggered a bit, and then strode forward. As weak mortals fell beside him in the battle of Armageddon, the warrior passed the carcasses with ease and never hesitated a moment. He did not dwell on those failures. Nothing could take him down. Nothing could pull him out of the heavens of success. Nothing could diminish his long-awaited zenith. But things could make him angry, dangerous, and volatile. His wrath was stored neatly within him until discouraging evils stepped forward to attempt to stop him.

Then the end would begin.

The rain cleansed her. Her eyes closed as the purification spread throughout her troubled mind. And serenity's grip swept her away from her world of darkness, and delivered her to a new world of change.

Within the world of reality, he was faced with those who unfortunately held him back. He wanted to do something. He wanted to get out and change the world. And a confrontation with the fools set it off. He turned his back and left it all behind. He turned his back, and faced something new. He turned his back and began a journey—one in the right direction—that allowed all evil to be left behind.

Let us stand up to the might of illusion! Fight it, resist it. What do you see? What *can* you see beyond that dark, dusky veil?

I have chosen to leave the game.
I have chosen to seep through the narrow cracks of the system. The codes, they mean nothing to me. These laws, they command nothing. This world, this world shall not bind me!

Never again will I make that mistake. I will no loner allow error to burgeon. It shall not flourish here, in my world. I shall stand above the veil, and keep inaccuracies far below me.

His disheartening decision shall be forgiven. I will annul my choice to be disdainful. This disappointment will be swept into the veil, and I shall help to restore a place of peace in this quadrant of Time.

The disappointment he has brought forth is a fine dust, one that etches shadow upon my heart. But I will clean it, and cauterize my pain.

When the end is in sight, who shall rise? Who shall rise, and choose to stand above the veil?

For such ignominy, bits of redemption
are present.

As the veil becomes weaker, the definite structures of darkness begin to crumble. My sad, cold world, situated within this passage of Time, was losing its stability. My divine mind, my mind structured with bravery and strong will, is ready to break out. My soul shall not be confined. My soul shall not be tortured. And I will prove it when this world of evil collapses.
When all collapses, the weak shall fall, and the strong will rise.

Time bleeds, and its golden blood oozes out of the boundaries of the veil. Time cannot be contained. My world shall dissolve. The veil has now been hit. It was my strength. I see around me, decay of this place. The repulsive flora is dying, the wind has ceased, and the veil... it is shaking with agitation. This golden, goo-like substance is covering the passage, and deteriorating all.

When all disappears, once the veil gives up, I know that I shall fade away as well. But I do not wish only to destroy this world of corruption. I must escape, too. I must return to my past world!

I thought. I thought a lot. I wished for more and more. I became more and more curious. I felt stronger and braver! I was ready to get out of my decrepit, hazardous chamber. I was ready to venture beyond.

There was a surfeit of mysteries to discover. And I was ready to escape and search for them! This denial, this fear, these flaws! They all must be left behind!

I looked toward the one exit of my dark place. The veil was getting angry. It did not want me to vacate. It would not let me break away from my troubles. But I was stronger! I had that will, that personality, that light! And with that, the veil caught fire. Black flames covered the shield, and penetrated the darkness and illusion.

Violet ashes lay at the gateway of reality and illusion. I stood, and proceeded toward the exit. I was going to leave this world stained gold. A white light poured into my cavern, the cavern I was about to leave behind. I rapidly kicked the soot aside and emerged from the bleeding home of evil. Reality's light was unbearably blinding. A tear, stricken with gold, leaked out into the new world of light that awaited me. An elation sat upon the blinding horizon of light.

About the Author

Nicholas Gupta draws his inspiration from visual images and sounds while crafting words that become his stories. Often, listening to eclectic styles of music, Gupta transforms mental images into written words that take the reader to extraordinary destinations. Written at just fourteen years of age, his first novel *The Unknown Species*, carried readers to a fantasy world of self-discovery and enlightenment. Enjoying acting and classic piano, and still attending high school, Gupta draws upon daily events and interpersonal relationships to inspire his creativity. Here, the young author used every day social interactions with friends to provide theme, texture and rhythm for *Secrets of the Veil*.

Printed in the United States
215709BV00001B/1/P